4x7=28
4x8=32
4x10=40
5x1=5
5x2=10
5x3=15
5x4=20
5x5=25
5x6=30
5x7=35
5x8=40
5x9=45
5x10=50
6x2=12
6x3=18
6x4=24
6x5=30
6x6=36
6x7=42
6x8=48
6x9=54
6x10=60
7x1=7
7x2=14
7x3=21
7x4=28
7x5=35
7x6=42
7x7=49

MATH ATTACK!

Joan Horton

Pictures by Kyrsten Brooker

Melanie Kroupa Books

Farrar, Straus and Giroux New York

In loving memory of my parents,
Lillian Fox Crane and Seymour Crane
—J.H.

For Colette and Jessie
xox —K.B.

It was Monday at school and our teacher, Miss Glass,
Announced, "Now it's time for arithmetic, class.
Can somebody tell me what's seven times ten?"
She was looking at me when she said it again.

I was thinking so hard all my circuits were loaded.
Then all of a sudden, my brain just exploded
And numbers flew out of my head by the score.
They stuck to the ceiling; they bounced off the floor!

Kids in the classroom dived under their chairs.
Some pushed through the hall and flew down the stairs.
"Enough," yelled Miss Glass. "You're disrupting the class."
She ducked as more numbers went whizzing on past.

The next thing I knew, I was sent to the nurse
"Before," said Miss Glass, "matters get any worse."

The nurse checked my throat, then peered in my ear.
"Oh my!" she exclaimed. "Now what have we here?
I'm afraid it's a case of arithmetic strain—
One that, no doubt, has scrambled your brain.

"How did this happen, exactly? And when?"
I told her, "It happened on seven times ten,"
But as soon as I said it, it started again!

Numbers flew out of my head as before.
"Gangway!" cried the nurse
As she dashed through the door.

But like a volcano that's blowing its top,
I kept spewing numbers. They just wouldn't stop.
They swept through the school, both the front and the back,
And the principal shouted, "We're under attack!"

At Precinct Eleven, Sergeant O'Toole
Was dispatching a unit to check on the school.
"Report of a math attack, Second and Main.
They say there's a kid with a scrambled-up brain."

The cruiser arrived and it screeched to a halt.
Young Officer Green and his partner, Kuralt,
Asked, "How did this happen, exactly? And when?"
I told them it happened on seven times ten,

But as soon as I said it, it started again!
Numbers swarmed out just like bees from their hives.

Everywhere, numbers were tumbling down—
On the school yard and houses and streets of the town.
They halted the traffic; horns started blaring.
Dogs began barking and townsfolk stood staring.

Suddenly telephones jingled and jangled
As numbers and overhead wires got tangled.
A man in a phone booth who tried calling home
Was connected, instead, to a sled dog in Nome.

To add to the racket, the clock in the tower
Was crazily bong-bonging every which hour,
For sixes and sevens had climbed from its base
To join the twelve numbers that circled its face.

Meanwhile as Millie, the grocery store clerk,
Was ringing an order for old Mrs. Burke,
Hundreds of numbers, piled high in a cart,
Leaped onto the shelves, giving Millie a start.

There they changed prices on jellies and jams,
On pickles and peppers and yogurt and yams.
Even the sticker on Mrs. Burke's bread
Was now reading ten trillion dollars instead.

Back at the school, the Channel 8 News
Arrived with their TV equipment and crews.
"We're live at the school," the anchorman said.

The camera zoomed in for a shot of my head.
"How did this happen?" he asked me. "And when?"
I told him, "It happened on seven times ten,"

But as soon as I said it, it started again!
Numbers flew out of my head helter-skelter.
The anchor and cameraman scrambled for shelter.

MATH ATTACK

Slate 1397   Take 17

3 0 4 6 5 3 2

At that very moment, the National Guard
Completely surrounded the school and the yard.
A whirlybird chopper flew low overhead.
I groaned and I wished I had stayed home in bed.

"It's hopeless," I muttered. "I'll never remember
The seven times table I learned in September."

That's when I heard it—a strange whirring sound
As gears in my head started spinning around.
My brain was computing. I tried once again
To remember the answer to seven times ten.

"Eureka, I've got it! I know it!" I said,
Just as the answer shot out of my head.
Then like a rocket on Fourth of July,
A towering seventy lit up the sky.

"Three cheers!" yelled the crowd. "At last," Miss Glass sighed.
"Ten-four," said the cops. My classmates high-fived.

I was ready the next day at school when Miss Glass
Announced, "Now it's time for arithmetic, class."
Hooray, bring it on! I thought, eager to start,
Certain I knew the times tables by heart.

My brain was unscrambled and working just fine
UNTIL Miss Glass said . . .

"What's eleven times nine?"

Distributed in Canada by Douglas & McIntyre Ltd.
Color separations by Chroma Graphics PTE Ltd.
Printed and bound in China by South China Printing Co. Ltd.
Designed by Irene Metaxatos
First edition, 2009
1 3 5 7 9 10 8 6 4 2

www.fsgkidsbooks.com

Library of Congress Cataloging-in-Publication Data

Horton, Joan.
    Math attack / Joan Horton ; pictures by Kyrsten Brooker.— 1st ed.
        p.   cm.
    Summary: When arithmetic strain scrambles a student's brain, no one in town is safe
from the numbers that go flying out of the child's head.
    ISBN-13: 978-0-374-34861-8
    ISBN-10: 0-374-34861-8
    [1. Arithmetic—Fiction.   2. Numbers, Natural—Fiction.   3. Stories in rhyme.]
I. Brooker, Kyrsten, ill.   II. Title.

PZ8.3.H78753 Mat 2009
[E]—dc22
                                                                        2006048774

3×1=3   4×1=4   5×1=5   6×1=6   7×
3×2=6   4×2=8   5×2=10   6×2=12
3×3=9   4×3=12   5×3=15   6×3=18
3×4=12   4×4=16   5×4=20   6×4=24
3×5=15   4×5=20   5×5=25   6×5=30
3×6=18   4×6=24   5×6=30   6×6=36
3×7=21   4×7=28   5×7=35   6×7=42
3×8=24   4×8=32   5×8=40   6×8=48
3×9=27   4×9=36   5×9=45   6×9=54
3×10=30   4×10=4   5×10=50   6×10=60